BLIPP

It was dusk at the Temple of Tunes. The entire Blippian Tribe was gathered for the Blessing of the Splingtwangers, in the presence of the Eldest One, her Council and the Musical Inquisitor . . .

On Planet Blipp, beyond the stars, beyond the sun and moon,
The world was ruled by music – but tradition called the tune.
The Ancient Songs of ages past were all that could be heard,
And no one was allowed to change a single note or word.

To write a tune was heresy, to play it even worse,
And anyone who improvised was scowled upon and cursed.
For years untold the Temple walls had rung to songs of yore –
Until the day a brave young groob named Sprocc rewrote the score.

Sprocc wasn't strong, or worldly-wise, just thirteen standard years,
But in his heart there surged a tune that conquered all his fears.
He took his trusty Splingtwanger, and though he knew 'twas wrong,
He cranked the volume up to ten and played a Brand New Song.

THE WORST BAND IN THE UNIVERSE

Graeme Base

For James, Katherine and William
and for Robyn, with love

Harry N. Abrams, Inc., Publishers

Sprocc
Member of Blippian Tribe
Instrument: Splingtwanger
Profile: Highly creative; potential Innovator
(presently under FTWDASD* surveillance)

Eldest One
Leader of Blippian Tribe and Supreme Ruler
of Federation of Tuneful Worlds (FTW)
Instrument: Ceremonial Splingtwanger

Musical Inquisitor
Galactic Supervisor of AudioSocial Discipline
and Commander in Chief of FTW ProdMen
Instrument: Splingtwanger (complete with
KnobbagePlus® accessory kit and chrome inserts)

Breather
Member of Pthwwwr Tribe
Instrument: Pthwwwrtian Snortlebone
Profile: Initiate of the Year, m2944.3
Suspected Innovator (file no. 13133)

Stickman
Member of United Stickpersons Collective 4.2
Instrument: Self-powered Filuvian MegaStix®
Profile: Medium-sentient percussion-based life form
Suspected Innovator (file no. 774)

Skat
Ex-member of Blippian Tribe (banished m2948.8)
Instrument: PowerAxe (illegal Splingtwanger/Matrix hybrid)
Profile: Failed initiation, Blipp m2948.7
Known Innovator (file no. 338): last sighted, Squaag 45.65.9.1

ButtonPusher
Member of Midimoog Tribe
Instrument: All bU.Mff compatible keydevices and
associated NrD electro-sonicware
Profile: B.S. (SonicEngineering), Univ. of GalSec14

Prodmen
Non-sentient techno-organic drones trained to
detect non-FTW approved vibrations and destroy
offending audio sources

Spotted Glerch
Highly evasive auto-morphing (shape-changing) life form
wanted by FTWDASD for breaches of AudioCodes 4457.7,
968.2 and 273.665
(please report sightings to your friendly neighborhood ProdCenter)

* FTWDASD: Federation of Tuneful Worlds Department of AudioSocial Discipline

The Musical Inquisitor was grobulous with rage.
"It's Banishment for you!" he snarled. "Remove him from the stage!"
A squad of ProdMen scuttled up and grabbed Sprocc by the scruff,
But as they made to drag him off a voice rang out, "Enough!"

The Eldest of the Eldest Ones, the Wisest of the Wise,
Rose slowly to her feet and studied Sprocc with ancient eyes.
"This lad is not a criminal," she finally declared.
"His heart is true – just out of tune. I say he shall be spared."

The crowd was in an uproar. The Inquisitor saw red.
But judgment had been given; there was no more to be said.
The Inquisitor was brought to heel – a sharp humiliation.
Repressive Tyrants: yet to score. Round One to Innovation!

When everyone had gone, the Eldest One took Sprocc aside.
"My son, you have a special gift, but one that you must hide.
Our world is not yet ready for the songs you wish to sing,
Be patient, Sprocc, for comes the day your music will take wing."

A sudden pang of sadness seemed to cut her to the core.
"Another young and restless soul has trod this path before:
A boy named Skat – he had the gift – a youngster just like you.
If only he had waited . . . There was nothing I could do."

Later that evening, Sprocc found himself at Planet Blipp
Provincial SpacePort . . .

That night, beneath a violet moon, our hero Sprocc was blue.
Although he'd not been Banished, life on Blipp for him was through.
He gazed up at the endless stars that wheeled above his head.
"I've got to find a place where I can play my songs," he said.

He thought of Skat, a troubled soul cast out from all he'd known,
A martyr for his music, somewhere out there, quite alone.
Perhaps he'd found another home, another place and time,
A world where Innovation wasn't thought of as a crime . . .

Just then, from far across the vale, he heard an Ancient Song,
A tune he'd known since childhood. He began to sing along.
But all at once inside his head he felt the music change –
Unbidden, Innovation had begun to rearrange!

The harmonies soared skyward as his heart took up the beat;
Echoes of the Universe, the rhythm of the street.
The joy of making something new, the impulse to create:
Sprocc's music meant the world to him – yet now it sealed his fate.

At last he stopped and looked around, and slowly shook his head.
"This planet's lost the plot," he sighed. "Its spirit's cold and dead.
There's more to playing music than the notes upon the page.
I have to call the tune myself, or else forsake the stage."

A SpaceBus heading off-world was preparing to depart;
Sprocc climbed up to the entry hatch with sad and heavy heart.
He turned and looked at Blipp, his home – it struck a poignant chord –
Then took a deep, determined breath and boldly stepped aboard.

SQUAAG

The Arrivals Hall at Planet Squaag Intergalactic SpacePort . . .

The moment Sprocc arrived on Squaag, he felt a sudden chill,
As if a silent hand had caused the airwaves to stand still.
No melody; no harmony; no tune or chord or song:
A total lack of music – there was clearly something wrong.

He powered up his Splingtwanger, the output set to low,
And strummed an Ancient Melody that everyone would know.
But instantly a squad of ProdMen scuttled into sight,
And headed straight for Sprocc, who stood in bafflement and fright.

A stranger who'd been watching Sprocc from far across the hall,
Moved quickly to his side and pulled him back against the wall.
She hit the entry panel on a vacant MTB.*
"It seems you have a problem, friend. You'd better come with me!"

The stranger pressed a button and the booth began to glow.
The fast-approaching ProdMen seemed to suddenly go slow.
Sprocc felt his body hovering, his head was filled with light,
Then in a blinding flash the SpacePort disappeared from sight.

*Matter Transfer Booth

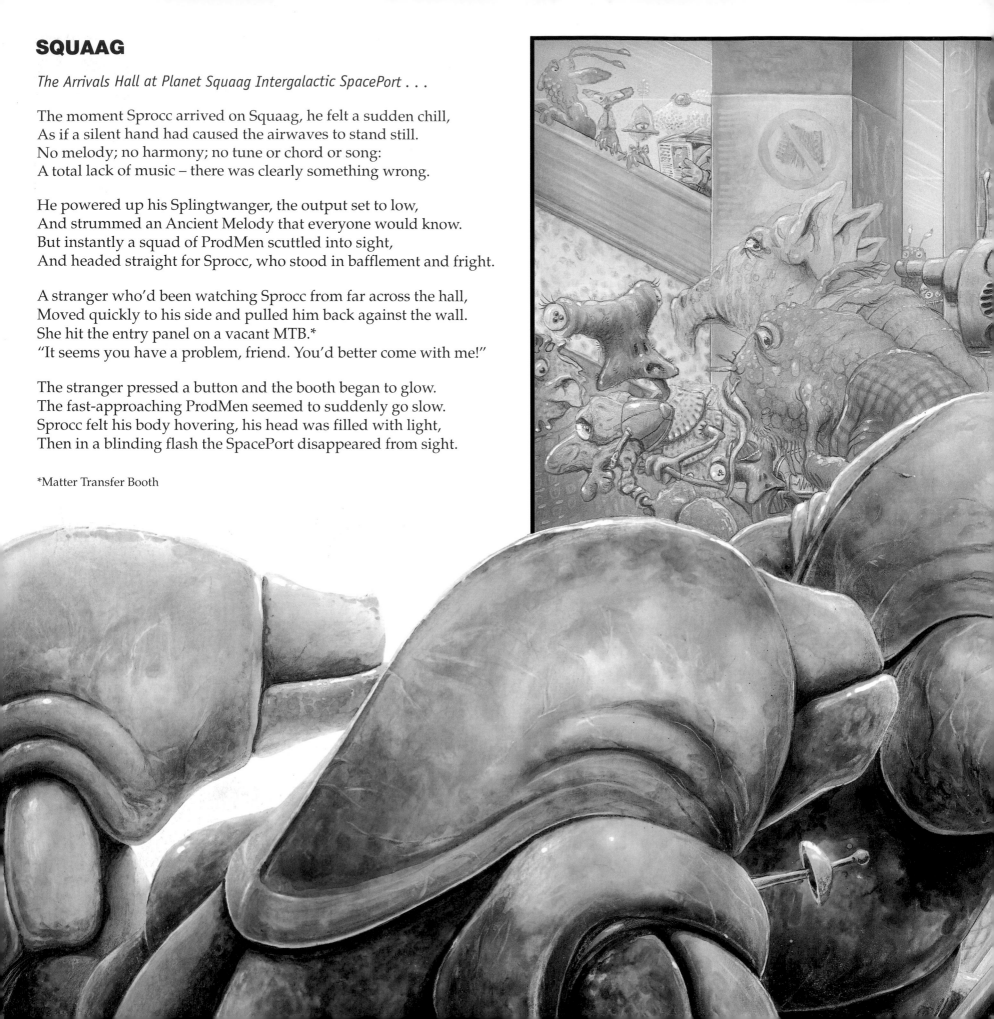

Sprocc reappeared in Sector 8, the low-life end of town.
The stranger let him stabilize, then looked him up and down.
"You must be new around these parts, or froozled in the head.
Performing with no license? Groob, right now you should be dead!"

"A license?" Sprocc was overwhelmed. "But why? Whatever for?"
"To keep us quiet! Rules are Rules – there's several thousand more:
Restrictions on recording, total bans on playing live,
All reggoid beats prohibited. No rok, no phfunk, no jyve."

"*No music . . .*" Sprocc stood dismally, head hanging in the rain,
His dreams of sonic freedom washing slowly down the drain.
"Cheer up." The stranger took his arm. "It's not as bad as that.
There's music here all right. Come on, I'll show you where it's at!"

She led him down dark alleys flanked by walls of PlastiRock,
Until they reached an unmarked door. The stranger gave a knock.
A secret code was verified, a password softly said,
Then down into the underworld young Sprocc was duly led.

A flood of music met his ears, so rich, so warm and deep,
The likes of which he'd never heard beyond the realm of sleep.
He felt himself enveloped in its magical embrace,
A smile that spoke of utter joy upon his upturned face.

The stranger led him through the hubbub toward a corner seat,
Where sat a massive CrustoPod she wanted him to meet.
"This lump is known as Stickman." (Stickman grinned a toothless grin.)
"And I, my friend, am Breather. Welcome to the World Within!"

That night Sprocc played his music as he never had before,
A sea of sound that rose and fell upon a rhythmic shore.
"Nice meshing, Sprocc-groob!" Stickman called. "You've really got it down!
This joint ain't heard a mesh like this since SkatMan came to town."

"You've heard of Skat! Is he on Squaag? I can't believe it's true!
I heard about him back on Blipp. He's just like me and you!"
But Breather shrugged: "I saw him once, a year or more ago.
I heard that he had traveled on, but no one seems to know."

Just then they felt a shudder, followed by a muffled roar.
A mass of rocks and rubble flew across the cavern floor.
A gaping hole. A searing light. The sound of stomping feet.
And with a roar a dozen ProdMen burst in from the street.

"Come on!" yelled Breather. "Time to split. This gig is getting rough!
These groobs look like they want to play, but I've had quite enough!"
Sprocc tried his best to follow but the rubble made him trip,
And all at once he felt himself held in a viselike grip.

The Musical Inquisitor sneered cruelly at his prey.
"My dear young Sprocc, we meet again. . . . This really makes my day!
Still making up our little tunes? Tut, tut, you cause me pain.
This time I'll have to see to it you never play again.

"Bring out the Bulk Eraser! We've an *Innovator* here,
Who thinks he has some Talent. Let us make it disappear —"
A sudden twist, a well-aimed kick, he feinted toward the right,
And Sprocc was racing up the street and off into the night.

Sprocc found the others waiting for him further up the lane.
"These raids are getting worse," said Breather. "Snoutface strikes again.
I wish we could get out of here, those ProdMen are such creeps,
But off-world tickets don't come cheap – looks like we're here for keeps."

An AutoDroid came skittering along the alleyway,
A roll of posters bouncing in its general-purpose tray.
It quickly slapped a poster up, glanced back along the street,
And darted off again upon its spindly, metal feet.

"The Worst Band in the Universe. Does Your Band Make the Grade?
First Prize: a Trip to Alpha 10, All Expenses Paid!
All Life forms Free to Enter. See below for Where and When.
You've Gotta Play to Get Away. It's Party Time Again!"

"The Worst Band?" chortled Sprocc. "Hey guys, this gig sounds pretty weird!"
But Breather told him here on Squaag the title was revered.
"A name to wear with pride, my friend, a truly worthy goal –
Who'd want to be the 'Best Band' in this grobulescent hole?"

Sprocc read the bit again about the trip to Alpha 10.
A chance like that was just too good – it might not come again.
He turned back to the others: "Well, we've nothing much to lose –
We'd better start rehearsing if we're going to win that cruise!"

The venue was a warehouse down in Sector 84.
The glowing Competition Host was waiting at the door.
"Step right this way, my grooblets. Let the Tournament begin!"
Sprocc thought he saw the slightest wink. "And may the Worst Band win!"

Inside they found a mass of musos meshing all at once –
A crodulous cacophony of clicks and snorts and grunts.
A band of Bogloids, heaps of Gleeps, a nest of HydroBugs,
Some Pangazordan Pongobums, a squeebling of Sluggs.

A family of Frooblesnags, Centaurans by the score,
A pair of Long-eared SlaterMen, a Giant Omnivore.
Such fabulous diversity – to name them all would spoil it –
And they were just the life forms who were queuing for the toilet.

Our heroes struggled through the crowd to SoundStage 42,
And kicked off with a trucking song that everybody knew.
The Host declared them winners of their class in Section One.
They moved on to the Second Round – the contest had begun!

For seven days and seven nights the Competition raged,
The most bizarre display of Innovation ever staged.
At last the hall fell silent; every band had done its worst.
They waited now with bated breath to find out who'd come first.

The Host stepped to the microphone, a wild look in his eyes:
"The judge has reached a verdict! Let us see who's won the Prize!"
He held aloft an envelope, and ripped it clear in two.
"The winner is . . ." he paused and looked around. "Why, Sprocc – it's you!"

The Worst Band in the Universe! They staggered back in shock.
"We've won the Competition! We are *outta* here!" cried Sprocc.
They whooped and yelled like crazy things, they leapt in sheer delight.
"No time for that!" the Host declared. "You've got to catch your flight!"

He led them quickly from the stage straight to the waiting ship.
"It's set to automatic. Just sit back, enjoy the trip!
If I were you I'd get some rest, you've quite a ride in store.
Be seeing you around, I guess . . ." He grinned and slammed the door.

Deep space, a few light-hours later . . .

The Band was watching TriVee* on the main transmission screen,
(A sitcom starring some new band from Alpha 17)
When suddenly the Host appeared – that glowing, golden smile –
"This program has been terminated. Do not touch your dial."

He flashed a set of perfect teeth, the smile became a laugh,
And then a dreadful, cackling howl that split his face in half.
The golden mask turned inside out, revealing in its stead,
The Musical Inquisitor! "Surprise, surprise!" he said.

He looked at Sprocc. "Now there's a face I've seen somewhere before.
You thought you had me beaten? Well, let's even up the score.
Prepare Ye for Oblivion, you innovative scum!
Your feeble tunes are all played out – and now my time has come!

"I have a dream, a Brave New World, where every note is fixed.
All tunes shall be performed in C, the Ancient Songs remixed.
A realm of sonic purity; the purging of creation.
And absolutely, positively *zero* Innovation!

"Of course, these new arrangements mean some changes at the top.
The Eldest One has had her day. She's ready for the chop . . ."
"You leave her be!" yelled Sprocc, but the Inquisitor was gone,
His laughter slowly fading as the spaceship hurtled on.

A minute later sirens blared; the seat-belt sign flashed red.
"ALL CREW PREPARE FOR HYPERJUMP," the AutoPilot said.
And then a void . . . a sense of loss . . . the future flashing by . . .
The ship leapt ninety light-years in the blinking of an eye.

They reappeared in orbit round a planet small and green.
"A jungle world," the read-out told them. "WasteDump B19."
A warning buzzer sounded. "WASTEPOD 7 CLEAR TO GO."
A jolt; and they were falling to the unknown world below.

*Three-Dimensional Television

WASTEDUMP B19

The Silent Swamp . . .

"Where are we?" muttered Breather as they struggled from the Pod.
"Some kind of jungle," Sprocc replied. "It sure feels pretty odd."
He gazed up at a foreign sky, a swirling, starless dome.
"One thing's for sure," he sighed. "We're all a long, long way from home."

They waded from the WastePod. Sprocc looked nervously around.
"I'd swear the jungle's listening, just waiting for a sound."
"This place has got me spooked," said Stickman. "How about a song?"
He tapped his sticks and hummed a tune. "Come on, guys, sing along!"

At once a dozen creepers slithered toward them from the trees.
"They're searching for the sound!" Sprocc whispered. "Everybody freeze!"
They stood as still as statues while around them swayed the creepers –
A terrifying real-life game of jungle finders-keepers.

Some unseen creature made a noise, an injudicious squeal.
The creepers pounced upon it, and the squeal became a meal.
The Band looked on in horror as the vines devoured their prey,
Then with a shudder turned and tiptoed quietly away.

And so to the vast junk piles of WasteDump B19 . . .

They crept along in silence; not a whisper, not a word.
Poor Stickman didn't dare to *think*, in case the creepers heard.
But finally the jungle thinned, they stepped into the light,
And found spread out before them an extraordinary sight.

A vast metallic landscape met their disbelieving gaze:
An interstellar junkyard disappearing in the haze.
A figure sat there watching them. "And what do we have here?
Another bunch of froozled groobs: must be that time of year."

A hundred other aliens were perched amongst the junk,
All kinds of musos: neutro, alloid, hyper-rap and phfunk.
But one was clearly in command – he spoke from where he sat.
"This here is WasteDump B19. And I, my friends, am Skat."

"It's Skat!" cried Sprocc, "I can't believe . . . It's really you . . . Oh wow!"
Skat watched with mild amusement, then he gave a mocking bow.
"And you, no doubt, are winners of a certain talent quest.
The Worst Band in the Universe? Ah yes, I might have guessed.

"Don't look surprised. You're not the first. This happens every year.
The thrilling win, the cheering crowds – and then you disappear.
We've all been there before, my friend, from old hand to beginner,
So welcome to the Worst Band Club – where everyone's a winner!"

The Band was stunned. Poor Stickman wept. Sprocc, too, was close to tears.
To think this vile deception had been going on for years!
"There must be some escape!" he cried. "Some spaceship we can use.
The Eldest One's in danger. There's no time for us to lose!"

"Be cool," said Skat. "So what? Who cares? It isn't our concern.
Remember you've been Banished, groob. No refund. No return."
Sprocc shook his head. "You're kidding, right? There's got to be a way.
The Universe needs saving, Skat! You can't sit there all day!"

"Hey, zip your lip!" Skat snapped at Sprocc. "*I'm* head-groob on this rock."
"Then how about you show a little leadership?" said Sprocc.
Skat's face betrayed a sudden rage. He raised his PowerAxe.
Sprocc's fingers gripped his Splingtwanger, the volume set to MAX.

But suddenly a snakelike shadow fell across the scene.
"Look out! A Gulper!" someone cried. Sprocc saw a flash of green.
Skat hammered on his PowerAxe – a massive pulse of sound.
Sprocc heard a SPLAT! and bits of creeper rained down on the ground.

Skat flicked the PowerAxe to OFF and slung it by his side.
"The Gulpers hear your every sound – there's nowhere you can hide.
My PowerAxe alone can keep the writhing horde at bay.
That's why I'm boss!" He glared at Sprocc, then turned and strode away.

When Skat had gone, a ButtonPusher waddled from the crowd.
"Er, hi," he mumbled. "Look, I wouldn't dare say this aloud,
But, well, I have this theory – though of course I may be wrong . . ."
He handed Sprocc a drawing. "*It's a ship that sails on song.*"

"A music-powered spacecraft?" Breather froobled through her snouts.
"It's possible, I guess," she shrugged. "And yet I have my doubts . . ."
"Skat says that it will never fly," the little guy confided.
"We'll try it!" Sprocc declared at once. "The matter is decided!"

Six weeks later . . .

The task was huge, the concept vague, the physics somewhat moot,
But once the seed of hope was sown it gradually took root.
They labored with the flame of freedom burning in their hearts,
A hammer, seven drill bits and an endless source of parts.

And slowly from the rubble grew a glorious creation:
A flimsy pile of rusted junk – the means of their salvation.
"You'll never make it fly," said Skat. "And even if you do,
The Gulpers will devour the lot – and take you with it, too!"

"You're right," said Sprocc. "Without your help we'll never get away.
But if this works we'll send a rescue ship without delay."
Skat turned on Sprocc in anger: "Who asked *you* to interfere?
We don't want you to save us! Can't you see we're happy here?"

"You're *happy* here? When every note you play could be your last?
When people live in fear of sound?" Sprocc looked at Skat, aghast.
"I really thought you'd help us, Skat, for everybody's sake.
I thought you were a leader, not a loser. My mistake."

Skat stared at Sprocc. His face went pale: the truth was all too stark.
Then silently he turned away. Sprocc's words had found their mark.
They watched him go. "This isn't good," said Stickman with a groan.
"At least you tried," said Breather. "Looks like we are on our own."

Lift-off Day . . .

At last the ship was finished. Sprocc called everyone around.
"All right," said Sprocc, "I'll count you in, then you guys make some sound!"
They climbed aboard and set the sails to capture every note –
A gallant bid for freedom in a tiny, homemade boat.

"Let's mesh!" cried Sprocc. The music flowed, the sails began to fill,
But from the jungle swarmed the Gulpers, closing for the kill.
"We need more power!" Breather yelled. "The EQ's going to blow:
The treble's overloading and the bass is way too low!"

"Transposing to a higher key!" Sprocc shouted from the bow.
"Let's try F sharp!" he cried and cast the line off from the prow.
The spaceship slowly swung around and lifted from the ground.
"We're taking off! It really works! A ship that sails on sound!"

But even as he spoke the Gulpers reached out to the ship,
Enveloping the vessel in their vegetably grip.
Poor ButtonPusher tumbled from his perch atop the mast.
The sonic sails flapped uselessly. The ship was sinking fast.

Then came a sudden blast of sound. The Gulpers writhed and squirmed.
"It's Skat!" cried Sprocc in wonderment. The sonic tide had turned!
Skat hammered on his PowerAxe, the Gulpers split asunder –
And Sprocc and crew soared skyward on a rolling wave of thunder.

Skat watched until the ship had gone, a tiny speck with wings.
"Hey Buttonhead, what say you make another of those things?
But this time make it really big, with lights and lots of chrome.
The Universe needs saving, groobs! It's time we headed home!"

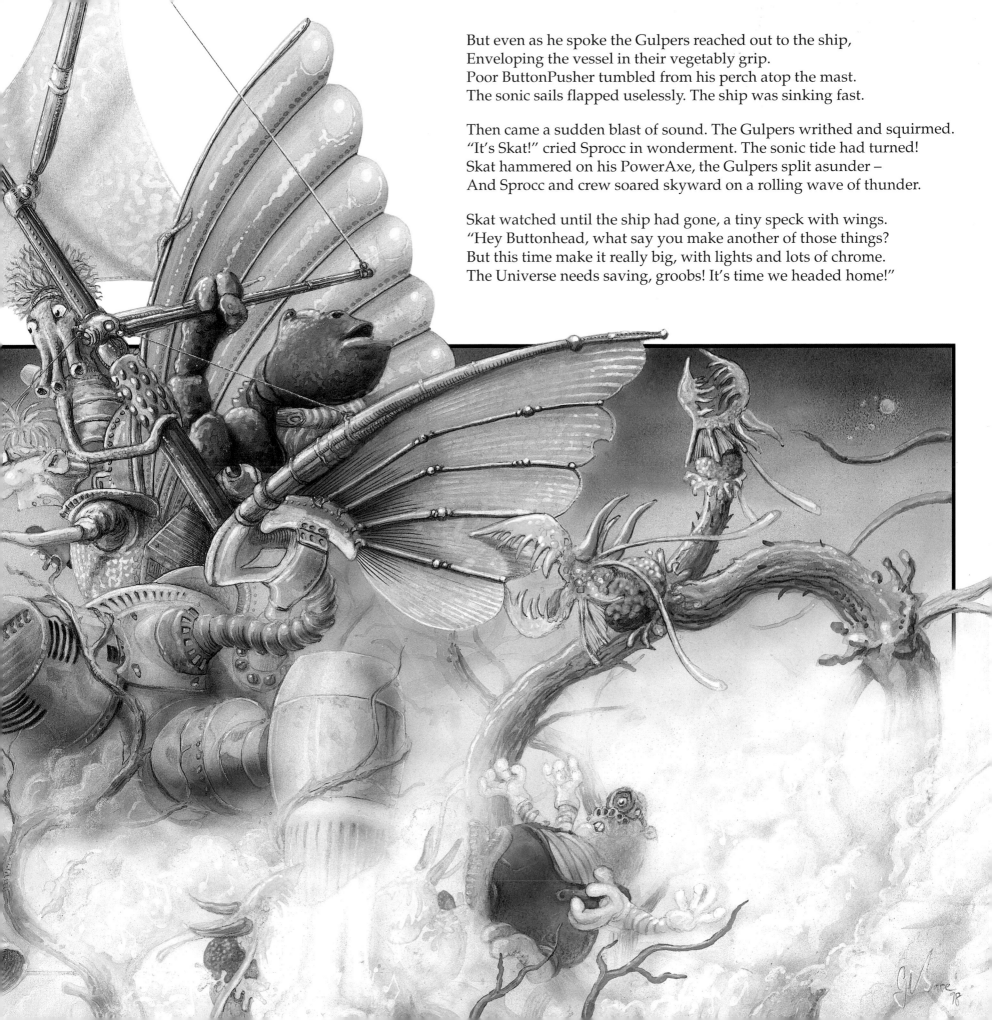

BLIPP

On Sprocc's home planet, a year had passed . . .

Beneath a dark, forbidding sky that spoke of storms and rain,
The Blessing of the Splingtwangers was underway again.
A squad of ProdMen, grim and silent, faced the restless crowd.
The Musical Inquisitor stood arrogant and proud.

"For far too long the Tuneful Worlds have wallowed in decay,
Bereft of moral principles, with none to show the way.
The Eldest One is old and weak – it's time she stood aside.
From now on *I'm* the Ruler of the Universe!" he cried.

The Eldest One rose slowly and looked deep into his eyes,
But all she saw was emptiness, depravity and lies.
She turned to face the audience. "Well, what say all of you?
Is this the one to lead us? Is he virtuous and true?"

The crowd glanced at the ProdMen and looked nervously away.
It seemed that the Inquisitor was going to win the day.
He stood before them unopposed – the president-elect.
Then suddenly a voice rang out: "Your honor, *I* object!"

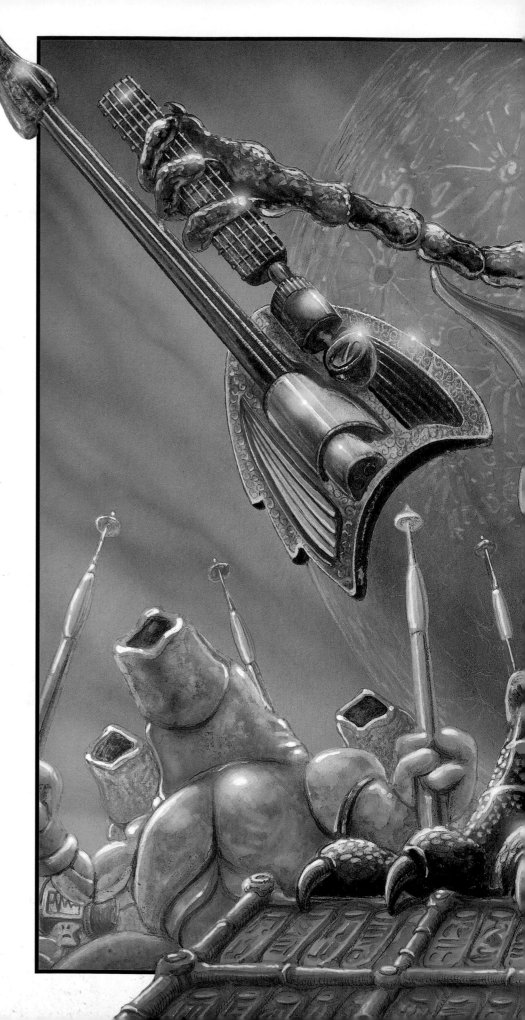

The Musical Inquisitor looked sharply down the aisle.
Sprocc stood there with his Splingtwanger and answered with a smile.
"Hello again. Remember me? You've met my friends before . . .
It seems that we are just in time to settle an old score!

"I exercise my Ancient Right, in keeping with Tradition –
The Ruler of the Universe must face some competition!"
The Musical Inquisitor rocked backwards on the stage.
"You dare to challenge me?" he shrieked, in shock as much as rage.

"You got it, Snoutman," Sprocc replied and switched to overdrive.
"The Worst Band in the Universe is coming to you *LIVE!*"
He rattled off a stunning line that sent the ProdMen reeling:
A triple-octave mega-riff with whammy bar and feeling.

"Well put," remarked the Eldest One. "This calls for a reply."
She turned to the Inquisitor. "I trust you're going to try?"
But all at once his face had paled. He stood there, hesitating.
"Come on now," said the Eldest One. "Don't keep your public waiting!"

A wave of panic crossed his face; a look of wild despair.
He searched within for talent and discovered nothing there.
Then through the Temple came a voice; a child, as clear as day.
"Look, Mommy!" said the little voice. "The funny man can't play!"

The people saw the child was right. He couldn't play a chord –
The Musical Inquisitor was nothing but a fraud.
He stood there in his impotence, their laughter in his ears,
And deep inside a madness grew that drowned out all the jeers.

"Go on and laugh!" he snarled at them. "Go on and have your fun.
For soon you'll know the sound of fear. This show has just begun!
You've made a fatal error, Sprocc. You've got me all annoyed.
If I can't rule the Tuneful Worlds, *then they shall be destroyed*!"

He pressed a secret button on his built-in microphone,
And suddenly his spaceship took a life all of its own.
It reared above their heads, a diabolical machine –
The biggest hi-fi system that the world had ever seen.

A lightning bolt lit up the sky. He held aloft a tape,
And thrust it in his Splingtwanger. The crowd tried to escape.
But instantly there came a noise that shook them to the bone:
A numbing flood of drivel – Random-Access DigiDrone.

The people staggered in the aisles, some fell upon the ground,
So mindless was the music, so monotonous the sound.
Sprocc tried to play his Splingtwanger, but soon was overcome.
He slumped against the speaker stacks, his mind and fingers numb.

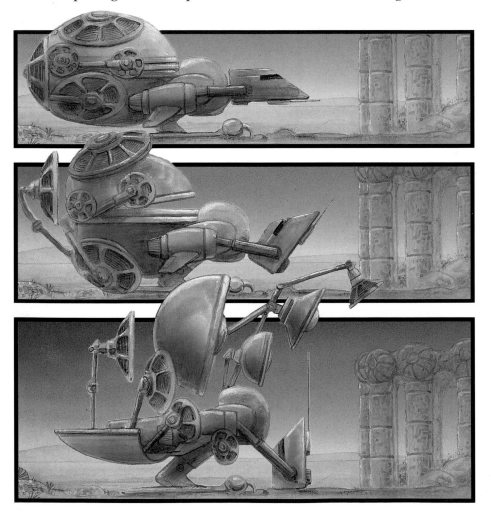

Then suddenly a ship appeared, like some enormous bat.
It skidded to a screeching halt and from it bounded Skat!
"Behold the Lost Musicians of the Universe!" he cried.
"You've played your last, Inquisitor. There's nowhere you can hide."

They stormed the giant speakers but the droning forced them back.
Their instruments fell to the ground; their hearts and minds went black.
"You fools!" cried the Inquisitor. "No one can stop me now.
This is the Final Chorus – and the last note is KA-*POW*!"

Then all at once a chord rang out, a clear and ringing tone,
That soared above the blandness of the awful DigiDrone.
All ears turned to the Eldest One: her Splingtwanger had spoken.
The darkness seemed to clear away. The evil spell was broken.

"Arise!" she cried. "The hour has come. Together we must fight.
Let Ancient Song and Innovation finally unite!"
The crowd took up their instruments and rallied to the call –
The Lost Musicians, Blippians, united one and all.

Sprocc played his trusty Splingtwanger, the throttle open wide,
The Worst Bands in the Universe all meshing by his side.
The sound that they created pierced the droning like a knife:
The eager blade of constant change; the cutting edge of life.

The Musical Inquisitor began to gag and choke,
As overhead the giant hi-fi billowed clouds of smoke.
His Splingtwanger exploded. Tangled tape flew everywhere.
A frightful squeal of rending steel, then silence filled the air.

The Temple lay in ruins. Sprocc was nowhere to be seen.
But then a muffled groan was heard from where the stage had been.
Sprocc staggered from the wreckage and the waiting crowd went wild.
The Eldest One embraced him. "Welcome home, my son," she smiled.

The Musical Inquisitor sat sobbing on the ground,
The remnants of his spaceship lying scattered all around.
His dreams of domination fled like shadows in the sun.
The rain had stopped. The clouds rolled back – a new day had begun.

"Rejoice!" exclaimed the Eldest One. "Rejoice in our salvation,
For thanks to Sprocc, the cosmos has escaped annihilation.
Repression has been vanquished by the forces of creation –
The armor of Tradition and the sword of Innovation.

"The right to play new music lies with every generation,
Regardless of their vocal range or rhythmic inclination.
The future lies before us, filled with boundless variation.
Lift up your voices! Sing your songs! This calls for Celebration!"

THE END

Library of Congress Catalog Card Number: 99–20968

ISBN 0–8109–3998–3

First published in 1999 by Penguin Books Australia Ltd

Published in 1999 by Harry N. Abrams, Incorporated, New York

Special thanks to Silicon Graphics for computer hardware support

Printed and bound in Australia

 Harry N. Abrams, Inc.
100 Fifth Avenue
New York, N.Y. 10011
www.abramsbooks.com

WORST BAND IN THE UNIVERSE
The Mesh

In a world that's given up listening
In a world that just won't hear
You've got to believe in one thing
Got to sing it loud and clear

Everybody needs the freedom
To be who they are

In a world that's under an ancient curse
The first will be last and the last will be first
And a group of young groobs
Could do much worse
Than be the Worst Band in the Universe

There's a groove on Alpha Centauri
There's a rap on Gamma 9
There's a song in every story
There's a rhythm in every rhyme

Sing your song
You're free to be who you are

In a world that's under an ancient curse
The first will be last and the last will be first
And a group of young groobs
Could do much worse
Than be the Worst Band in the Universe

LET'S GO! (BACK TO THE BIG BANG)
The Omnivores

Just beyond the edge of infinity
Back before the dawning of time
History was yet to get on with it
Stars had not yet started to shine
Deep in the primordial nothingness
Deep within the bubble and strife
Lies a point of cosmic significance –
Nothing less than the secret of Life

We've got to know
So we're heading right back
To the start of the show
Let's Go! Back to the Big Bang

Will the Universe go on forever
Expanding out into infinite space?
Or will it all just squish back together?
These are questions we all have to face
There's only a billion years left on the clock
When the big hand points up
It's the end of the race

We're flying blind
Unless we get back to the beginning of time
Let's Go! Back to the Big Bang

FADE AWAY
Pthuii

When the winter rains have come to stay
Everyone could do with some time away
Pick out a star that's new
It's easy, there're quite a few
And teleport yourself on holiday

Fade away
Suspended in motion
In a molecular potion
Slap on the sun lotion
And slide into the ocean

Long ago we would have gone by sea
Days and nights that dragged on endlessly
Flying was something new
But now you just join a queue
And let your body simply cease to be

Fade Away
Suspended in motion
In a molecular potion
Slap on the sun lotion
And slide into the ocean
Your brain's disconnected
Your atoms are collected
But until we get the process perfected
All damage claims will be rejected

PLANETFALL
The Mesh

I've been across I've been across
This old universe
More than I could care to tell
Lightspeed has had had had had
It's effect on me
I've b-b-been away for too long

When I left to find find find find
Some peace of mind
Baby said she said to me
Take care and bring back
Bring bring back a star for me
Don't be-b-be away for too long
Don't be-b-be away for too long
I've been away but I'm coming back home

The sky is beginning to glow
I'm coming home coming home
There's not that much longer to go
I'm coming home
Home is where I want to be
I've changed and I want you to know
I'm coming home coming home

Nothing can prepare you
Nothing can prepare you
For the rush of Planetfall

I've seen the sun I've seen the sun
Sunset setting sun
On so many different worlds
But I long to feel old Sol
To feel sun sunny Sol again
I've b-b-been away for too long
I can see the rings of Saturn now
They're spinning spinning just for me
I've b-b-been away for too long
I've been away but I'm coming back home

I'm tired. Oh I've tried to be strong
I'm coming home coming home
I know this is where I belong
I'm coming home
Home is where I want to be
I've seen the light

And I know I've been wrong
I'm coming home coming home

Nothing can prepare you
Nothing can prepare you
For the rush of Planetfall

I'm coming home

The sky is beginning to glow
I'm coming home coming home
There's not that much longer to go
I'm coming home
Home is where I want to be
I've seen the light
And I know I've been wrong
I'm coming home coming home
Nothing can prepare you
Nothing can prepare you
For the rush of Planetfall

ANCIENT MELODY #42
(traditional instrumental)
*Anonymous**

90 LIGHT-YEARS FROM THE SUN
The Mesh (featuring Skat the Axeman)

Sitting on a rock
Beneath a strange and empty sky
Just me and my splingtwanger
I sit and wonder why
Why I have to live here
In this silent wilderness
Why I had to play the songs
That got me in this mess
Living, living on the run
Living 90 light-years from the sun

Songs about the universe
Rhythms of the street
Lyrics sung without a sound
A groove that has no beat
Echoes from the dawn of time
A tune you'll write next week
All of it connected
It's the thread that we all seek
We're living, living on the run
Living 90 light-years from the sun

Why'd I play the music
That I heard inside my head
When I knew the songs
They wanted me to play instead?
Questions with no answers
If your heart is made of stone
All I know is music
Is the one thing that I own
I'm living, living on the run
Living 90 light-years from the sun

Listen to the echoes from the distant drums
Listen to the rhythm
Something this way comes
Trying to find the chords
That set the world apart
Bring us back together for a brand new start
But until then we're living, living on the run
Living 90 light-years from the sun

ALPHA 10 (semi-instr. version 57.7)
*The Amazing Centrifugal Blortcrooners
of Alpha 10*

Alpha 10, Alpha 10
Alpha 10, Alpha 10
Alpha 10, Alpha 10
etc.

W.Y.S.I.W.Y.G.
The Omnivores

Good to see you here my love
I've missed your bulging eyes
Come a little closer now
I've got you a surprise
It's nothing much – a simple gift
To show my love for you
A box of slimy squirtlegreebs
In sticky yellow goo

Kiss me, give me a hug! I long to feel loved!
Well I'm cheap to feed coz I eat only slops
And I never get sick coz I've had all my shots

I've got three strong arms
One enormous nose
Nine left feet with twenty-seven toes
I've got no brain but that's the way it goes
What You See Is What You Get
W.Y.S.I.W.Y.G.
Who needs hair? What's the use of teeth?
Mine all fell out
And there's no more underneath
But if you love me take me as I am
What You See Is What You Get
W.Y.S.I.W.Y.G.

Pay no heed to scabs and warts
Mere failings of the skin
Beauty, so the sages say
Lies buried deep within
Still you ought to wash your hands
You don't know where I've been

Kiss me, give me a squeeze!
I'm begging you please!
I could sleep in the yard
Or wherever it suited
And I won't get into fights
Coz I've already been neutered
(no problem there)

I've got three strong arms
One enormous nose
Nine left feet with twenty-seven toes
I've got no brain but that's the way it goes
What You See Is What You Get
W.Y.S.I.W.Y.G.
Who needs hair? What's the use of teeth?
Mine all fell out
And there's no more underneath
But if you love me take me as I am
What You See Is What You Get
W.Y.S.I.W.Y.G.

* In keeping with Blippian tradition all
  performances of Ancient Melodies are
  made anonymously.